DIAMOND Hunter

By John Lockyer
Illustrated by Lorenzo van der Lingen

DIAMOND Hunter

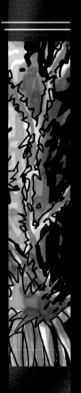

Cruz felt the crumpled map in his pocket and remembered the strange little curio shop where he'd found it. The shop sold all kinds of things from Egyptian artefacts, shimmering silk, cheap statues of emperors, queens and kings, to jewellery, gold, and old books and papers.

The map was in a small, glass case. It was drawn in hieroglyphics. The shopkeeper said it had belonged to ancient explorers. Cruz didn't believe her but he was curious and bought it anyway. Later, when he looked closer at the map, he realized there was a tiny key to the hieroglyphics. The map was of the old city, now in ruins. Among the ruins was a narrow alley. And in the alley was a secret door that supposedly led to a lost treasure.

LED TO A LOST TREASURE

3

Cruz stood alone in the alley. He had been up and down the narrow passage many times and was getting hungry and tired. He'd looked carefully at the crumbling walls and crawled along the cobbled path searching for the secret door, but so far hadn't found it.

It was getting dark and cold. He tightened his coat and looked at the map again. He knew he was in the right place. He could feel it. Frustrated, however, he decided to give up for the day.

As he turned to leave, he was drawn to an archway that was littered with stumps of broken statues. He hadn't thought much about it before, but looking at it this time sent shivers down his spine. Cruz crawled in behind the pieces and pressed himself against the wall. It suddenly creaked and crashed inward.

Clarify

FRUSTRATED

A, B OR C?

A weary

B feeling dissatisfied –
     unable to progress

C sad

EMOTIONS

What emotions might Cruz be experiencing?

excitement	anxiety
tranquillity	sadness
fear	happiness
	apprehension

Cruz fell backward in a shower of dust and sand. He coughed and shook the dust off his head. The wall creaked closed behind him. Was this the secret doorway? It was too dark to see. He coughed again then froze. He heard sounds coming from somewhere.

Cruz searched for a way out. He looked up. No windows. No doors. He ran his hands around the walls. All stone. No. He felt cloth – heavy, woven curtains. He pushed them open and leaped into the space behind them, falling into a small, dark chamber. His hands, searching the walls, touched a lever. He pushed it up. The room suddenly glowed bright white. Cruz stared. There were no walls, no ceiling, and no floor. Just white space.

Clarify

CHAMBER

A, B OR C?

A flowerpot

B enclosed space

C small porch

QUESTION?

Cruz felt himself moving. He moved his foot, but felt nothing solid. He reached out a hand. His arm twisted and corkscrewed but without pain. He pulled his hand back and frowned. What was happening? How was he moving? Where was he going? Had he found the secret door? What would he find?

The white light began to dim. More walls and another curtain appeared, this time accompanied by a soft buzzing. He pulled the curtain aside and the buzzing became louder. There was an oval-shaped door at the end of a dim corridor. Pulling it open, he realized that the buzzing had become voices – strange voices.

IMAGERY

Use the imagery of
the text to create
your own picture.

HIS ARM TWISTED
AND CORKSCREWED

Predict

What do you think Cruz
might experience next?

Cruz moved toward the voices. Leaving the shadows, he stared at what he saw before him.

Hustling and bustling around him were creatures – multi-armed robots, multi-headed robots, multi-legged robots. There were hairy beings, scaled beings, and green-fleshed beings. There were winged creatures, fanged creatures, and horned creatures. They moved around the room, touching, holding, grunting, and inspecting strange metals, minerals, materials, and machinery. They waved arms, shook heads, and shouted at each other. What business were they at? Some seemed to be buyers. Some seemed to be sellers. It was a bazaar – a market place – but in another time! Is this where the treasure was?

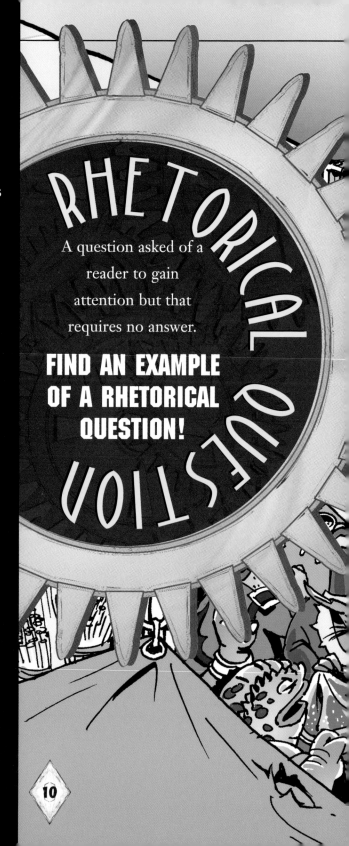

RHETORICAL QUESTION

A question asked of a reader to gain attention but that requires no answer.

FIND AN EXAMPLE OF A RHETORICAL QUESTION!

IT WAS A BAZAAR

Cruz stopped at the nearest table. "What's going on?" he asked a bald, scaled creature. "Why is everyone in costume?"

The creature opened its lipless mouth, hissed, and shoved him away. Cruz fell into the crowd. Warm bodies and cold bodies pushed against him. He pushed back then pulled his hands away.
The creatures weren't in costumes. They were real!

Cruz wriggled and squirmed. There were hands all over him. He felt for the map in his pocket. There had to be something on it that would explain where he was, but the map was gone.
He checked his other pockets. Nothing. He looked around quickly.

Had one of the creatures stolen it? Cruz frowned. He was afraid. He looked for the doorway, but couldn't see it. Pushing and shoving, he forced his way through the crowd. "A doorway?" he shouted. "Where's the doorway! Someone please show me where it is?" No one answered him. He stared at the sea of strange faces. "I'm not like you," he shouted. "I only came for the treasure. I don't belong…"

Setting:

What words would you use to describe the atmosphere of the place where Cruz is now?

A	thrilling	F	grotesque	J	weird
B	inviting	G	uncanny	K	bizarre
C	pleasant	H	warm	L	freakish
D	frightening	I	impressive	M	mysterious
E	creepy			N	unearthly

Something touched his shoulder. Cruz twisted round. A black, shiny robot with three arms and one red eye stood beside him. It pointed to a mirror on a wall. Cruz looked at the mirror then he looked at the robot. The robot pointed to the mirror again. Cruz looked into it and touched it. Immediately a voice said, "Welcome, humanoid. Welcome."

Cruz gasped. The robot was speaking through the mirror.

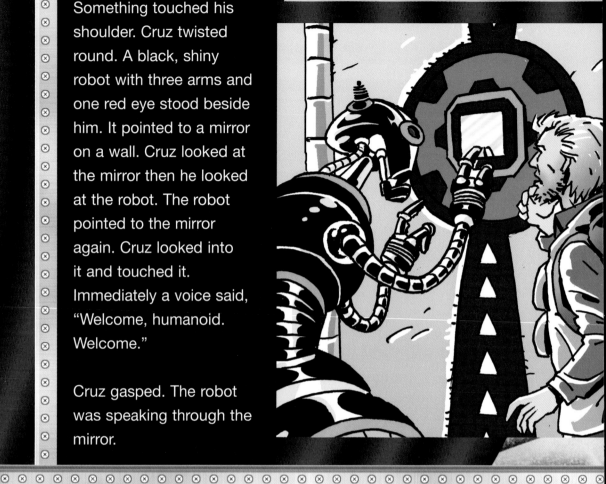

Clarify

HUMANOID

A, B OR ?

A robot

B doll

C a being with the appearance of a human

The mirror seemed to be a voice decoder of some sort. It picked up the robot's voice and continued decoding as they moved toward an odd-looking machine.

"This is Lapis," said the robot, touching the strange funnelled gadget on the table. "Lapis will give you what you want. Tell me, humanoid. What is it you want?"

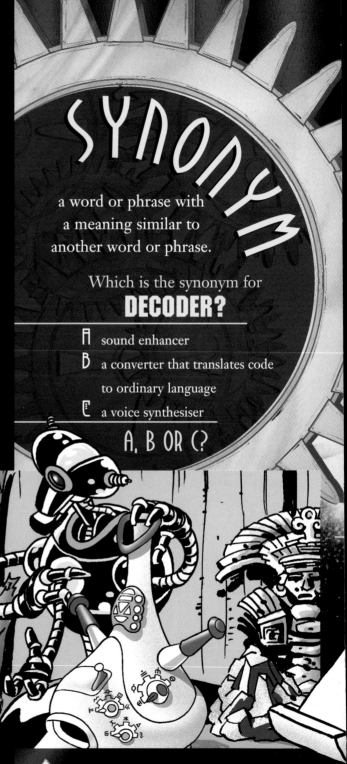

SYNONYM

a word or phrase with a meaning similar to another word or phrase.

Which is the synonym for
DECODER?

A   sound enhancer

B   a converter that translates code to ordinary language

C   a voice synthesiser

A, B OR C?

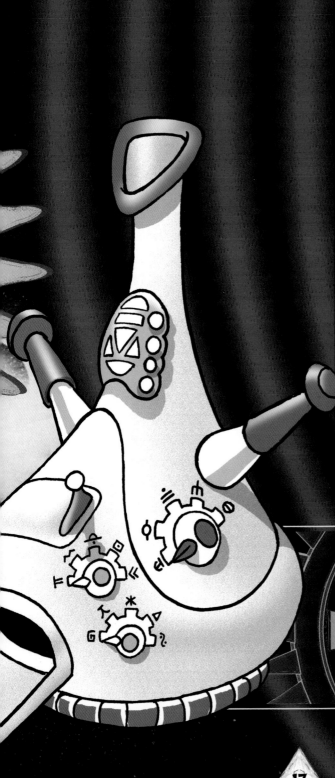

Cruz glanced around again. "The oval door…" he started to say, then stopped. His eyes narrowed. "Did you say ANYTHING?"

The robot nodded. "Of course."

Cruz smiled. "What about diamonds?"

The robot's eye flashed. "Diamonds, rubies, emeralds, sapphires, whatever. But you have to stay here with us in order to have them. You see…"

Inference

What inference can you make about the character of Cruz?

Cruz raised his hand, interrupting the robot. "Diamonds," he said. "Just give me diamonds." Once he got the diamonds, he'd think of a way out of there.

"Diamonds it is," said the robot, tipping black powder from a pouch into what he had called Lapis.

Cruz frowned. "Diamonds can be made from that stuff?" he asked.

The robot nodded. "Once it took millions of light years, high temperatures, pressure, and carbon to form diamonds. Now I add the carbon and Lapis does the rest in seconds."

QUESTION?

Why do you think
Cruz said –
"Diamonds, just
give me diamonds?"

The powder disappeared and the robot fingered some dials on the funnel. It whirred, and wobbled, then was still. A moment later an oval stone rolled out of the funnel. The robot caught it and held it to the light. The stone glowed golden yellow. Cruz whistled long and low.

"A perfect canary diamond – 30 carats," said the robot, fingering the dials again. Golden diamonds popped out all over the place. Cruz laughed and scrambled to catch the three sparkling stones that the robot threw to him.

Lapis stopped whirring and the flow of diamonds halted. The robot collected and counted the newly formed gems. Cruz shuffled backward. His fingers curled around

the diamonds as he held them in his fist. He had to make his move. Spinning around, he pushed back into the crowd.

"Stop!" shouted the robot. "Come back! You don't understand!" But Cruz did not stop.

Character Profile:

HOW MIGHT YOU BEST DESCRIBE CRUZ?

A timid

B daring

C bold

D selfish

E greedy

F

G

H

?

Predict

What do you think will happen in the story now?

Once again the creatures pressed against Cruz. They forced him this way and that. He stumbled and fell to his knees. Heavy feet clomped all around him. He tried to stand up, but the bodies pressed him down. He heard the robot shouting, "Come back, humanoid!"

Cruz ducked under a table. On hands and knees, he crawled from table to table, searching the shadows for the doorway. Pausing to catch his breath, he was sure it was close by. But the robot was even closer. It thrashed and crashed around him.

"Foolish humanoid!" it cried. "You cannot leave here with the diamonds I gave you! We will make you one of us! You can have all the diamonds you desire."

Cruz crouched lower. He knew he had to make a run for it. The place and the creatures totally creeped him out. He breathed deeply and scurried out from under the tables into the shadows. His feet scraped across some stones.

Action and Response

Cruz stumbled and fell to his knees

The robot roared. Its red eye flashed. One black arm coiled and sprung after Cruz. Its metal fingers clutched at Cruz's shirt. Cruz wriggled free. "The doorway," he gasped. "It's here somewhere. I know it is."

The robot's fingers grasped at Cruz's shirt again. Cruz dropped one of the diamonds. It bounced back toward the robot, but Cruz didn't stop.

Then he saw the oval door. Skidding to a stop, he glanced back. The robot, red eye flickering, picked up the loose diamond and held it up to the light. It flickered fire and gold. Then the robot was moving again, shouting and stretching its tentacle arms toward Cruz.

FLICKERING

Cruz stumbled through the doorway and along the corridor. He entered the tiny chamber, pushed past the curtain and ran his hands along the wall until he found the lever. Flicking it down, he slumped to the floor. Then he saw the white light, heard the hum, and felt the motion. Still grasping the cold hard lumps in his hand, he breathed a little easier.

Within moments, the walls and curtains reappeared. Cruz got up slowly and leaned against the far wall. It creaked and opened. Cruz saw the broken statues and the alley. Sighing with relief, he pushed the door open wider and stepped around the broken statues. He had made it. And he had the diamonds to prove it.

Opening his hand, he saw that there were no diamonds, however. Only fine, black powder that sifted through his fingers onto the ground.

For a moment, Cruz was disappointed. But the thought of staying in that strange place for the rest of his life didn't appeal to him in the least. Not even a little bit. Not even if he could have all the diamonds he wanted!

He headed home to get something to eat.

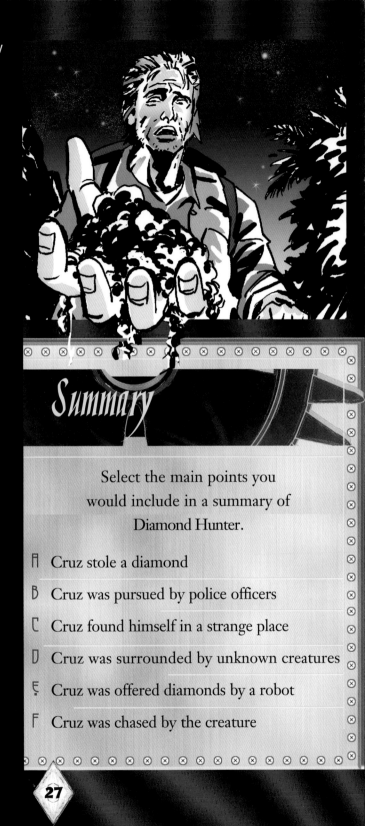

Summary

Select the main points you would include in a summary of Diamond Hunter.

A   Cruz stole a diamond

B   Cruz was pursued by police officers

C   Cruz found himself in a strange place

D   Cruz was surrounded by unknown creatures

E   Cruz was offered diamonds by a robot

F   Cruz was chased by the creature

THINK ABOUT THE TEXT

What connections can you make to *Diamond Hunter*?

NOT THINKING ABOUT CONSEQUENCES

FEELING ALIENATED

EXPERIENCING PANIC

BEING IMPATIENT

Text To Self

BEING GREEDY

BEING FOCUSSED ON TASK

BEING INTRIGUED BY A MYSTERY

FEELING STRANGE

FEELING FRUSTRATED

TEXT TO TEXT

Talk about other texts
you may have read that
have similar features.
Compare the texts.

TEXT TO WORLD

Talk about situations in
the world that might
connect to elements in
the text.

29

PLANNING A SCIENCE FICTION STORY

Decide on a storyline that has a problem and a resolution:

A diamond hunter is searching for diamonds.

He discovers another time and another world where robots using machines make diamonds in minutes.

He tries to take the diamonds back to the real world and creatures try to prevent him.

He has to find his passage back home.

The diamonds turn to carbon in his pocket as he travels back in time.

Think about
the characters:

Think about the way they
think, act and feel.
Make some short notes or
sketches.

obsessed with
diamonds

impatient

DIAMOND
HUNTER

doesn't
listen

thinks little of
consequence

aggressive

CREATURES
IN THE
WORLD
BEYOND THE
CURTAIN

cold and
uncaring

impulsive

unhearing

Decide on
the settings

SETTING A
Curio shop with Egyptian
artefacts, silk, statues,
jewellery, old books and
papers

SETTING B
Old ruins with broken
statues and a secret
door in a wall

SETTING C
Small dark chamber
with heavy curtains and
lever that when activated
transports occupant
through white glowing
light to other world

SETTING D
Bazaar in another time
and place with strange
metals and machinery
and alien creatures.

SCIENCE FICTION STORIES USUALLY FEATURE...

Scientific language and ideas

Imaginary or futuristic worlds

A fear of the unknown

A sense of being alien in a strange environment

Things that are not as they appear to be

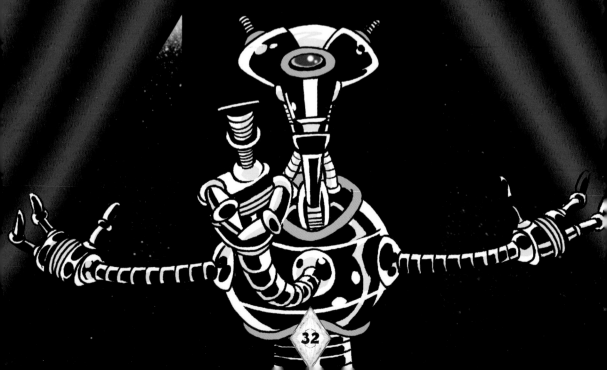